EARLY BIRD STORIES

Clumpety Bump

Early ★ Reader

First American edition published in 2023 by Lerner Publishing Group, Inc.

An original concept by Phil Allcock
Copyright © 2023 Phil Allcock

Illustrated by Richard Watson

First published by Maverick Arts Publishing Limited

Maverick
arts publishing

Licensed Edition
Clumpety Bump

Lerner Publications Company
An imprint of Lerner Publishing Group, Inc.
241 First Avenue North
Minneapolis, MN 55401 USA

For reading levels and more information, look up this title at www.lernerbooks.com.

Main body text set in Mikado a. Typeface provided by HVD Fonts.

Library of Congress Cataloging-in-Publication Data

Names: Allcock, Phil (Children's fiction writer), author. | Watson, Richard, 1980– illustrator.
Title: Clumpety Bump / Phil Allcock ; illustrated by Richard Watson.
Description: First American edition. | Minneapolis : Lerner Publications, 2023. | Series: Early bird readers. Green (Early bird stories) | "First published by Maverick Arts Publishing Limited"— Page facing title page. | Audience: Ages 5–9. | Audience: Grades K–1. | Summary: "Wally Wobblebottom likes to bring gifts to his friends. But his horse, Clumpety Bump, is not always helpful"— Provided by publisher.
Identifiers: LCCN 2021055148 (print) | LCCN 2021055149 (ebook) | ISBN 9781728438870 (lib. bdg.) | ISBN 9781728448398 (pbk.) | ISBN 9781728444598 (eb pdf)
Subjects: LCSH: Readers (Primary) | LCGFT: Readers (Publications)
Classification: LCC PE1119.2 .A453 2023 (print) | LCC PE1119.2 (ebook) | DDC 428.6/2— dc23/eng/20211202

LC record available at https://lccn.loc.gov/2021055148
LC ebook record available at https://lccn.loc.gov/2021055149

Manufactured in the United States of America
1-49674-49594-12/6/2021

EARLY BIRD
STORIES

Clumpety
Bump

Phil Allcock

illustrated by
Richard Watson

Lerner Publications ◆ Minneapolis

Clumpety Bump was a horse.

A lazy horse. A VERY lazy horse.

He didn't gallop. He didn't trot.

But he loved eating apples.

His owner, Wally Wobblebottom, liked to help people. He wished Clumpety would help him more.

But Clumpety was too lazy.

On Monday, Wally's friend Mrs. Grumble was ill. So he set off on Clumpety Bump to take her some grapes.

Wally said, "Let's go across that field, Clumpety. Clippity clop, don't stop!"

But Clumpety Bump thought,

"I can't be bothered!"

He nibbled the chewy, gooey grass

instead. Wally jumped up and down

but he squashed the grapes.

SPLAT!

"Oh no!" he muttered.

On Tuesday, Wally took some chocolates to his friend Jenny Penny.

Wally shouted, "Let's go across the stream, Clumpety. Slippity slop, don't stop!"

But Clumpety Bump thought,
"I can't be bothered!" So he drank
the dribbly, wobbly water instead.

SPLASH!

The chocolates floated away.

"Oh no!" cried Wally.

On Wednesday, they took some homemade jam to Wally's friend Tom Toe.

Wally cried, "Let's go over that log, Clumpety. Zippity zop, don't stop!"

But Clumpety Bump thought, "I can't be bothered!" He stopped to nibble some yummy, tasty leaves.

OUCH! Wally fell in some nettles and

the jam went everywhere.

"Oh no!" he yelled.

"I've had enough, Clumpety!"
Wally shouted.

"If you don't want to trot, gallop,
or jump, you can stay at home!"

On Thursday, Wally wanted
to take flowers to his friend
Ann Key. But he decided not
to take Clumpety . . .

He set off on his tractor instead.

BRRMMM
BRRMMM

But it got stuck in a big muddy puddle.

SQUELCH
SLURP

Wally tried to push it out, but
he slipped. "Oh no!" he groaned,
"I should have brought Clumpety!"

He went home to find Clumpety.

"I'm sorry I left you behind, Clumpety,"

said Wally. "But please, can you help me?"

Clumpety grinned.

He wanted Wally to be happy again.

So off they went. Clumpety galloped across the field and didn't stop to eat the chewy, gooey grass.

He splashed across the stream and didn't stop to drink the dribbly, wobbly water.

He jumped over the log and didn't stop to nibble the yummy, tasty leaves.

They soon reached Ann's house.

"Hello Ann," smiled Wally,

"I've brought you some . . ."

MUNCH!

"Oh no! Clumpety's eaten them!"

"Never mind!" grinned Ann, kissing him on the cheek. "Do you want to fetch an apple for Clumpety?"

"I can't be bothered!" replied Wally.
"Oh no!" thought Clumpety.

"Only joking!" grinned Wally.

And he gave Clumpety the crunchiest,

munchiest apple ever.

Clumpety Bump was a horse.

A lively horse. A VERY lively horse.
He liked trotting, jumping, and
galloping. And helping Wally.
And most of all, he loved eating apples.

Quiz

1. Clumpety Bump was a _____.
   a) Dog
   b) Horse
   c) Boy

2. What does Wally want to take to Mrs. Grumble?
   a) Grapes
   b) Flowers
   c) Apples

3. Who is Wally taking the chocolates to?
   a) Clumpety Bump
   b) Mr. Grumble
   c) Jenny Penny

4. Why does Wally leave Clumpety
   at home?
   a) Because he is too fast
   b) Because he wants to help
   c) Because he is too lazy

5. What does Clumpety get in
   the end?
   a) The crunchiest, munchiest apple
   b) Some jam
   c) A tractor

Leveled for Guided Reading

Early Bird Stories have been edited and leveled by leading educational consultants to correspond with guided reading levels. The levels are assigned by taking into account the content, language style, layout, and phonics used in each book. Visit www.lernerbooks.com for more Early Bird Readers titles!

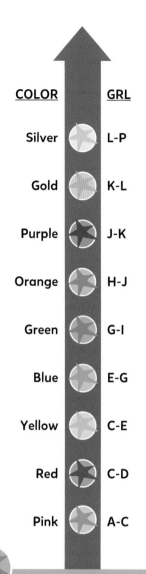

COLOR	GRL
Silver	L-P
Gold	K-L
Purple	J-K
Orange	H-J
Green	G-I
Blue	E-G
Yellow	C-E
Red	C-D
Pink	A-C